PEDRO GOES WILD!

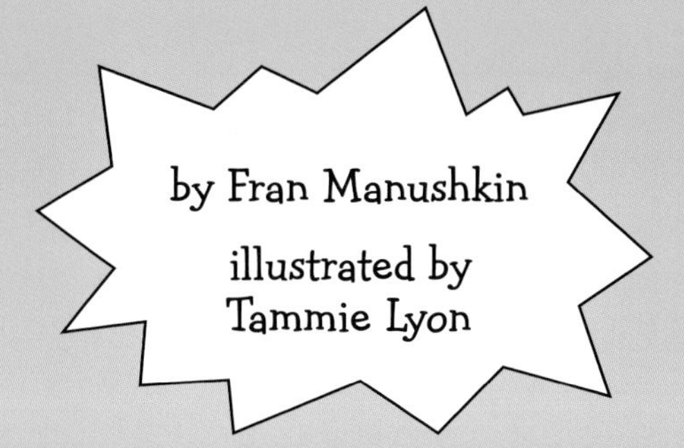

PICTURE WINDOW BOOKS
a capstone imprint

Pedro is published by Picture Window Books,
a Capstone imprint
1710 Roe Crest Drive
North Mankato, Minnesota 56003
www.capstonepub.com

Library of Congress Cataloging-in-Publication Data
Names: Manushkin, Fran, author. | Lyon, Tammie, illustrator. | Manushkin, Fran. Pedro.
Title: Pedro goes wild! / by Fran Manushkin ; illustrated by Tammie Lyon.
Description: North Mankato, Minnesota : Picture Window Books, [2019] | Series: Pedro | Summary: Pedro and his father go on a hike in the woods—where it turns out that Pedro knows a lot more about the plants and animals than his father does, but they both have fun anyway.
Identifiers: LCCN 2018054335| ISBN 9781515844501 (hardcover) | ISBN 9781515845638 (pbk.) | ISBN 9781515844525 (ebook pdf)
Subjects: LCSH: Hispanic American boys—Juvenile fiction. | Hiking—Juvenile fiction. | Fathers and sons—Juvenile fiction. | Forest animals—Juvenile fiction. | CYAC: Hispanic Americans—Fiction. | Hiking--Fiction. | Fathers and son—Fiction. | Forest animals—Fiction.
Classification: LCC PZ7.M3195 Pcd 2019 | DDC 813.54 [E] —dc23
LC record available at https://lccn.loc.gov/2018054335

Designer: Charmaine Whitman
Design Elements by Shutterstock

Printed and bound in the USA.
PA71

Table of Contents

Chapter 1
Take a Hike! 5

Chapter 2
Picnic Panic 13

Chapter 3
Here Comes a Storm! 18

Chapter 1

Take a Hike!

"It's a sunny day," said Pedro's dad. "How about a hike?"

"Cool!" said Pedro. "I love the woods. We can be wild."

“Don’t worry about getting lost,” said Pedro’s dad. “I’m a great hiker.”

“Good!” said Pedro.

They began to walk.

“These leaves are pretty,” said Pedro’s dad. “Let’s pick some for Mom.”

“Stop!” yelled Pedro. “That’s poison ivy.”

“Wow!” said Pedro’s dad. “That was scary.”

“Not as scary as bears,” said Pedro. “I hope we don’t see any.”

"Oh boy!" said his dad. "If I saw a bear, I would try flying away like that crow."

"That's not a crow," said Pedro. "It's a hawk."

"He's fierce!"
said Pedro's dad.

"For sure," said
Pedro. "Hawks like
to eat rats."

"Yuck!" said Pedro's dad.
"I wouldn't!"

"Let's run now," said Pedro.

His dad ran fast. Suddenly

he yelled, "STOP! I see a bear!"

The bear was . . . a sweet, fuzzy dog!

Pedro's dad laughed and laughed. So did Pedro.

Chapter 2
Picnic Panic

"Now, let's eat," said Pedro's dad.

"Your peanut butter sandwich is terrific," said Pedro. "Now, I need a drink."

“Uh-oh!” said his dad.

“I forgot to fill the canteen.”

Pedro asked, “Dad, did you ever hike before?”

His dad smiled. “A long time ago.”

"Let's give these ants a sandwich," said Pedro.

The ants ate all of it. They didn't need a drink.

They began walking again.

"Yikes!" yelled Pedro's dad. "Something big just jumped on my leg."

He ran in a panic and fell in a puddle!

“It’s only a frog,” said Pedro. “It can’t hurt you.”

“Oh my!” His dad laughed. “I am a terrible hiker.”

Chapter 3

Here Comes a Storm!

Pedro looked up at the sky.

"Uh-oh," he said. "A storm is coming! Let's hurry home."

“We came on this path,” said Pedro’s dad.

They began walking. It was the wrong path! Lightning started! And thunder!

“Don’t worry!” said Pedro.

“I think I know the right way.

But I can’t run as fast as you.

Can you carry me?”

“Sure I can,” said Pedro’s dad. He began running.

Uphill! Then downhill! And uphill again!

Pedro's dad was strong and fast. He ran like the wind.

"Go, Daddy!" yelled Pedro.

At home, Pedro's dad said, "I'm sorry I didn't know much about hiking."

Pedro shook his head. "Dad, you know the most important thing."

"What's that?" asked Pedro's dad.

"You know how to have fun!" said Pedro.

"I do!" His dad beamed.

They hugged on it.

PEPE
PEDRO

About the Author

Fran Manushkin is the author of Katie Woo, the highly acclaimed fan-favorite early-reader series, as well as the popular Pedro series. Her other books include *Happy in Our Skin*, *Baby, Come Out!* and the best-selling board books *Big Girl Panties* and *Big Boy Underpants*. There is a real Katie Woo: Fran's great-niece, but she doesn't get into as much trouble as the Katie in the books. Fran lives in New York City, three blocks from Central Park, where she can often be found bird watching and daydreaming. She writes at her dining room table, without the help of her naughty cats, Goldy and Chaim.

About the Illustrator

Tammie Lyon began her love for drawing at a young age while sitting at the kitchen table with her dad. She continued her love of art and eventually attended the Columbus College of Art and Design, where she earned a bachelor's degree in fine art. After a brief career as a professional ballet dancer, she decided to devote herself full time to illustration. Today she lives with her husband, Lee, in Cincinnati, Ohio. Her dogs, Gus and Dudley, keep her company as she works in her studio.

Glossary

beamed (BEEMD)—smiled widely

canteen (kan-TEEN)—a small portable metal container for holding water or other liquids

lightning (LITE-ning)—a flash of light in the sky when electricity moves between clouds or between a cloud and the ground

panic (PAN-ik)—a sudden feeling of great terror or fright, often affecting many people at once

poison ivy (POI-zuhn EYE-vee)—a shrub or climbing vine with clusters of three shiny, green leaves. Poison ivy causes an itchy rash on most people who touch it.

terrible (TER-uh-buhl)—very bad

terrific (tuh-RIF-ik)—very good or excellent

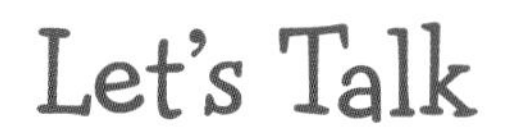

1. Who was better at hiking in the story? Explain your answer.

2. Pedro has a little brother named Paco. How would the story have been different if Paco had gone hiking too?

3. Do you think Pedro and his dad's day was a good day or not? Share details from the story to explain your answer.

Let's Write

1. Thinking about the story, list at least five reasons why people enjoy hiking.

2. Draw a map of hiking trails. Name your trails and include labels.

3. Pedro's dad thought a dog was a bear. Imagine they really did see a bear. Write a paragraph about what happens next.

JOKE AROUND

Which side of a tree has the most leaves?
the outside

Why did Humpty Dumpty have a great fall?
Because he enjoyed all the colorful leaves while hiking.

What did the hikers call the bear with no teeth?
a gummy bear

Have you heard the joke about the skunk and the hiking trip?
Never mind—it really stinks.

WITH PEDRO!

- Why was the pine tree sent to its room?
  It was being knotty.
- What did the lake say to the hikers?
  Nothing, it just waved.
- Knock, knock
  Who's there?
  Woods
  Woods who?
  Woods you like to go for a hike?
- Why are people who go hiking on April Fools' Day so tired?
  Because they just finished a 31-day March.

HAVE MORE FUN WITH PEDRO!

We started up the trail again.

"Let's sing a song," I said.

"How about 'I've Been Working on the Railroad?' " Mario asked. He stopped and picked up a rock.

For the next hour, we sang songs. We walked and walked up the hill. My feet hurt. I was hungry.

"Let's eat after we cross that stream," Mario said.

"I brought all the food," I said. "Just like we planned. It's in my backpack."

"Super," Mr. Zinger said. "And I brought trail mix for snacks."

ROCKS

We walked across the stream on a log. First Mario walked over.

The Spy looked in each direction before he crossed.

Bubbles took little ballerina steps across. She stood on the tips of her toes.

Woof swam across the stream and barked. "WOOF!"

It was my turn. I stepped on the log. OOPS! I slipped.

Oh no! My backpack fell off. It fell in the stream. I said a quick prayer. I asked Jesus to help us.

"I'll get it!" Mr. Zinger shouted.

I crossed the log and looked back. Mr. Zinger pulled my backpack out of the water. Water dripped out of the side. Mr. Zinger set it down.

I opened my backpack and peeked inside. “Our lunch looks terrible!” I cried. “The sandwiches are dripping. The cookies look like mud. All the food is wet! What will we do?”

"Jickle, ee, ee," The Spy said. He wrote notes in his book.

Then he set up the folding table. He spread out a red-checkered tablecloth. He opened his backpack. He pulled out three pizzas!

"Wow!" I said. "Thanks!" We all said a prayer. We thanked Jesus for the extra food.

"It looks like The Spy is prepared for anything," Mario said.

The Spy wrote more notes in his book.

After lunch, we packed our backpacks.

We started up the trail again. We hiked for hours.

Suddenly Bubbles sat down.

"What's wrong?" I asked.

Bubbles pulled off her ballerina slippers. "I'm getting blisters. It hurts every time I practice a jump. What will I do?"

The Spy reached in his backpack. He pulled out three pairs of shoes. "Jickle, ee, ee," he said.

"You brought extra hiking boots?" Mr. Zinger asked.

Bubbles picked the smallest boots. She tried them on.

"They fit!" she cried. "Thanks! Now my feet won't hurt."

I thanked Jesus for taking care of my friend.

We hiked all the way to the top of the hill.

"This looks like a good place to camp," Mario said.

Woof wagged his tail and barked. "WOOF!"

"We'll be able to see the comet from up here," I said. "Let's get our sleeping bags out. It's almost dark."

"I'll start a campfire," Mr. Zinger said.

Bubbles opened her pink sleeping bag. I opened mine. We set them close to the campfire.

The Spy started to unpack his backpack.

Rocks

“Mario, where’s your sleeping bag?” I asked.

Mario looked sad. “I forgot it. I wanted my backpack empty to collect rocks. I forgot to pack my sleeping bag.”

Bubbles practiced a pirouette. Then she sat down on her sleeping bag. I sat down on mine. We looked at Mario.

Then we looked at The Spy.

Rocks

The Spy unpacked his backpack. He pulled out a telescope. He pulled out wood for the fire. Then he pulled out two sleeping bags.

"Jickle, ee, ee," he grinned.

We laughed. "Be prepared!"

Mr. Zinger added wood to the fire. It was dark.

"It's cloudy tonight," Mario said. "Will we see the comet?"

We munched on The Spy's hot dogs.

"Let's sing more songs," I said. "Maybe the clouds will go away."

We sang "Row, Row, Row Your Boat" 30 times.

The Spy set up his telescope. Suddenly we heard snoring. We stopped singing.

"Mr. Zinger's asleep," I whispered. "He's tired from hiking all day."

"Bubbles is asleep too," Mario whispered. "She's tired from practicing pirouettes."

Mario and I sat on our sleeping bags. The Spy looked into his telescope.

I heard another snore. Mario was asleep too.

I rubbed my eyes. I wanted to stay awake to see the comet. But I felt so-o-o sleepy …

I fell asleep and started to dream. I dreamed Bubbles jumped over the comet.

"The comet!" The Spy shouted.

I woke up.

The Spy was excited. He forgot to speak in secret code. "Hey, everybody!" he shouted. "Wake up! I see the comet!"

I tried to jump up. My legs got caught in my sleeping bag. I fell down. I crashed into Bubbles.

"Hurry!" The Spy cried. "You'll miss it! The clouds are coming back!"

Bubbles tried to jump up. Her tutu got caught in the bag's zipper. R-I-I-P! "Help!" she cried. "I'm stuck!"

I grabbed the zipper. I pulled. “Come on!”

We stood up and bumped into Mario.

“Watch out!” Mario yelled.

Woof barked. “WOOF!”

We raced over to The Spy. We tripped over Mr. Zinger. Mr. Zinger was still asleep.

“Wha-what?” Mr. Zinger cried as he woke up.

“The comet!” we yelled.

We all ran over to the telescope. I peeked in first. “I don’t see it.”

The Spy looked in the telescope. He stood up and shook his head.

I looked up at the sky. “The clouds are back,” I said softly. “No comet.”

Drip. Drop.

"What was that?" Mario asked.

Drip. Drop. Splash.

"It's starting to rain," Bubbles said. "What can we do? My tutu will get all wet!"

The Spy ran to his backpack. He pulled out a pop-up tent.

"Jickle, ee, ee!" The Spy shouted. We ran inside the tent. The Spy carried in the telescope. Woof shook his fur. He splashed water on everyone. The Spy handed us all towels.

We sat inside and listened to the rain. Suddenly, I giggled.

"What's funny?" Bubbles asked. "I don't think anything's funny. My tutu ripped again. My feet are wet. And I didn't get to see the comet."

"It's funny how The Spy brought so much stuff in his backpack," I said. "Even a telescope and a tent. I thought it was silly. But it wasn't. He was the only one who saw the comet."

"You're right," Mario agreed. "I think we all learned an important lesson today."

Bubbles nodded and smiled.

Mr. Zinger nodded too. "From now on, we should always say, 'Jickle, ee, ee.' "

The Spy laughed. "Be prepared!"

Parable of the Ten Girls

Based on Matthew 25:1–13

Jesus told a parable:

Ten girls were invited to join a wedding feast. They needed lamps and oil to find their way.

Five girls were prepared, but five forgot the oil to put in their lamps. All 10 girls fell asleep waiting for the party.

When the time came for the wedding feast, only the five who were prepared could go to the feast.

Just like the girls who forgot the oil for their lamps, Bubbles, Suzie, and Mario forgot important things for their campout.

But The Spy was prepared. He was the only one who saw the comet.

The Bible says that Jesus will come back to earth someday. If we believe that Jesus died on the cross to forgive our sins, we will be ready to see Him when He comes. Let's be prepared to meet Jesus when He comes!

Hi!

Jesus died on the cross to forgive our sins. He'll come back to earth someday, so we need to be prepared. Here's one way you can put Jesus' Parable of the Ten Girls into ACTION!

Parables In Action

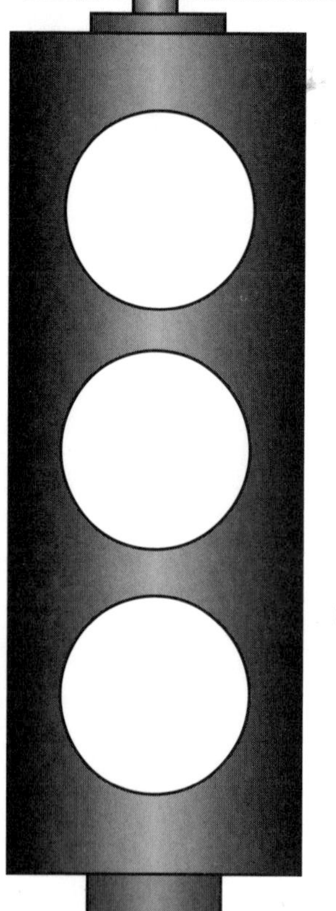

Get Ready. Spend time with other kids telling them about your best friend, Jesus.

Get Set. Fill an empty lunch box with things such as a video about Jesus, a storybook about Jesus, and stickers or small toys with Bible verses on them.

Go! Next time your friends come over, open the lunch box and share the things inside. Then your friends can be prepared to meet Jesus too!